THE
ALAMO
CAT

THE ALAMO CAT

WRITTEN AND ILLUSTRATED BY

RITA KERR

EAKIN PRESS Austin, Texas

Library of Congress Cataloging-in-Publication Data

Kerr, Rita.
    The alamo cat / by Rita Kerr. — 1st ed.
        p.   cm.
    Summary: Recounts the adventures of Ruby, a stray kitten adopted by the patrol rangers at the Alamo as their mascot.
    ISBN 0-89015-639-5 : $7.95
    1. Ruby (Cat) — Juvenile fiction. 2. Cats — Texas — San Antonio — Juvenile fiction. 3. Alamo (San Antonio, TX) — Juvenile fiction.
[1. Ruby (Cat) — Fiction. 2. Cats — Fiction. 3. Alamo (San Antonio, TX) — Fiction.] I. Title.
PZ7.K468458A1   1988
[Fic] — dc 19   88-3843
                                                                                 CIP
                                                                                 AC

*This book is dedicated to
my mother, Maya Wilson,
to Doug Kaetz,
and to cat lovers everywhere.*

Contents

Acknowledgments   vii

1   The Alamo Kitten   1

2   A New Home   12

3   Ruby's Big Surprise   18

4   Ruby's Kittens   28

5   Danger!   35

6   Ruby Defends the Alamo   40

Bibliography   49

All names of characters in this book, with the exception of Ruby the cat and her six kittens, are fictitious, and have no relation to the names of actual people.

Acknowledgments

The author wishes to express her appreciation to Charlene Eakin for her suggestions and expertise. Thanks goes to the teachers, librarians, and schoolchildren who showed an interest in *The Alamo Cat*. Special thanks goes to Charles Oaks and Doug Kaetz and the other dedicated employees who work at the Alamo. Thanks also goes to the librarians of the DRT Alamo Library: Sharon Crutchfield, Jeannette Phinney, Sandy Hall, Charline Pazliska, and Bernice Strong. The author is grateful to Dr. G. D. Norsworthy, San Antonio veterinarian, for his assistance and to artists Andy Johnson and Mary Toddes for their encouragement.

The author expresses her gratitude to the Daughters of the Republic of Texas for their preservation and upkeep of the Alamo and its history.

1

The Alamo Kitten

The night was warm and pleasant. Fleecy clouds drifted quietly across the moonlit sky. Ranger Zira was making one of his regular rounds of the Alamo grounds. Suddenly, he had a strange feeling he was being followed.

"Ruby, is that you?" he whispered softly into the darkness. There was no answer.

In his heart Zira knew it could not be Ruby, his beloved Alamo cat; she had been dead for over a year. But tonight Zira felt her presence so strongly that he could almost believe the stories that her ghost had been seen stalking the grounds of the old fort.

"Ruby, is that you?" he repeated his words.

Silence.

If Ruby's ghost was there, Zira could not see it. He sighed and continued down the path. The feeling that the cat was nearby was overpowering. Zira stopped and looked back again.

Nothing.

Zira walked to the *acequia,* the water canal, to look down into the murky waters where Ruby had drowned. The moon now cast a mysterious shimmer upon the courtyard. He remembered when the kitten first came into his life. Ruby had been so small — so frightened. Closing his eyes, Zira imagined he was back to that August night in 1981. The scene gradually unfolded before him . . . .

"Meow! Meow!" The faint cry came out of the darkness.

"What's that?" Zira mumbled to himself as he shined his flashlight slowly across the east wall of the Alamo. He heard the sound again. It now seemed to be coming from a large tree on his right. Beaming the light upward, Zira walked in that direction. He was directly beneath the tree when he saw the small, furry ball clinging to one of the upper branches. It was almost hidden by the thick leaves. As he stared at the spot, two large green eyes stared back at him.

The creature cried again. "Meow!"

"Why, that's a kitten! Are you stuck? Say, how did you get up there anyway?" Zira muttered, rubbing his chin thoughtfully. "My friend Kensey would know how to get you down, but I'm not calling him at this hour of the night. Besides, there isn't much we could do until morning." He zigzagged the beam of light across the branches. There was no way he could climb that tree — not without help. "Well, I must finish my rounds, kitty. Don't go away. Maybe I can think of something."

Zira could hear the kitten crying as he walked on down the path flashing his light into the dark shadows around the Alamo. He knew every nook and corner, each bush and water ditch on the grounds by heart.

In his years as night patrolman for the Alamo Rangers, the hallowed walls of the old church had become part of his life. A deep sense of pride swelled up inside of him when he remembered those brave men who died on March 6, 1836, defending the Alamo against General Santa Anna and his Mexican army. Zira felt a lump in his throat every time he read the names of those gallant heroes written on the plaques along the walls of the Alamo: William Barret Travis, James Bonham, Jim Bowie, Davy Crockett, and about 180 others. Zira felt honored to be a part of something so glorious to San Antonio and Texas.

Tonight Zira was not thinking of history. His thoughts were about the kitten in the tree. Once he completed his rounds, Zira went to his desk in the guard office in the old Long Barracks to make his hourly report. He automatically filled his coffee cup and reached for the lunchpail he brought to work each night. His wife Katee insisted that anyone who worked from midnight to eight in the morning and slept during the day needed a late snack. The Rangers on the eight-to-five and five-to-twelve shifts could eat their meals at normal hours, but Zira liked the third shift. He was a night person who needed little sleep. He did not mind eating at strange hours.

Zira's snack tonight was sliced chicken, cherry pie, and a carton of milk. Suddenly, he had an idea. If he could not get *up* to the kitten, perhaps he could get it to come *down.* With that thought and his thermos cup in his hand, Zira grabbed his pail and flashlight to go outside again.

Leaving the door slightly ajar, he retraced his steps. Zira heard the kitten's pitiful cries long before he reached the tree. He propped the flashlight against the trunk to send a beam upward.

"Come here, kitty. See what I've got?" Zira's friendly voice drew the hungry kitten from its hiding place among the leaves. It crept slowly toward the center of the tree. "So — you weren't stuck after all! Well, come on down."

Sinking its sharp claws into the soft bark of the trunk, the kitten edged its way slowly downward. Suddenly, it stopped and stared at him. Zira prayed hunger would overcome the kitten's fear of him. When it started down again he heaved a sigh of relief. Zira caught it by the nap of the neck when it was within his reach. The frightened creature hissed and spit, swinging its claws wildly in the air.

"Feisty little thing, aren't you?" Zira chuckled. He put the cat on the ground and took the milk carton out of his lunchpail. As he poured a little milk into his thermos cup, the kitten sat huddled at his feet. "Why, you're just a baby! Don't you know how to get the milk?" He decided the best way to show the creature was to rub some milk on its nose then poke its head into the cup. The kitten sputtered and choked but soon lapped the milk with its tiny tongue. The cup was empty in no time.

"You're a fast learner, kitty!" Zira said, picking up his gear. "Now, go find your mother. I have work to do."

He started toward the office. When he glanced back he realized the kitten was following him. "Get lost! Animals aren't allowed in here." Zira took two steps and stopped. The kitten was right at his heels. "Shoo! Go!" It did not move. Zira tried again. "Go away before something bad happens to you. Scat."

With that, Zira headed for the Long Barracks. There was no sign of the animal when he looked again. "I guess I know how to scare a cat," he muttered proudly.

Zira kicked the half-opened door with his foot and turned to his desk. To his amazement, there sat the cat! Before Zira could move, it leaped to the chair and upon his desk.

"Well, I'll be! How did you get in here?" Sinking into his chair, Zira stared at the kitten. It had a long tail and round little body. Its short, thick fur was a calico pattern of white and black and reddish-orange patches. A streak of white went from the center of the kitten's forehead to the tip of its pointed nose. Its enormous green eyes reminded Zira of bright searchlights. Zira had never seen such strangely colored eyes. As he opened his pail and unwrapped the sliced chicken, the Ranger wondered how the poor little thing had gotten into that tree.

The sight of Zira's food was too much for the kitten — it went wild! "All right, I'll give you some," Zira grumbled. The kitten swallowed the tiny bites of chicken and begged for more. Soon it was all gone. "I guess you know you've eaten my supper, but you'll not get my pie!"

The kitten was not concerned. It was busy taking a bath. Zira could not keep from smiling. "Now aren't you something? You act like you belong here, but you don't! Question is: What do we do with you? I can't take you home with me. We can't have pets in our apartment. And, as far as I know, no animals have ever been allowed to live on the Alamo grounds — except maybe horses and cattle during the war. You don't want me to get in trouble do you?"

The kitten meowed softly as it licked Zira's finger. "Say, I don't know much about cats. I don't know if you're a girl or boy. How about me calling you Ruby until I find out? Ruby sounds better than kitty, doesn't it?"

For an answer Ruby twitched the tip of her tail, closed both eyes, and proceeded to roll into a furry ball. Zira shook his head. "Hey, you're in the middle of my papers. Give them here. I have work to do." The kitten half opened one eye as Zira yanked out his report. The sound of his scratchy pen blended with the loud purring noise coming from the cat. It was sound asleep.

When he finished writing, Zira poured himself another cup of coffee and stared at the small ball of fluff in front of him. "You look so comfortable, I guess you can stay the rest of the night. But out you go when daylight comes. I don't want to lose my job over a cat."

The next morning Zira carried the kitten to the back gate before the day shift came to work. "Get lost, kitty. Go find yourself a home. You can't stay here." He turned on his heels and walked away. When he looked back, Ruby was gone.

Zira did not speak of the cat to anyone until that evening. He told his wife about his visitor before he went back to work.

"Well," she said. "If you fed that kitten, don't be surprised if it comes back tonight. I packed cookies and another carton of milk along with the rest of that chicken for your supper. Should I put in something else in case it does return?"

Zira laughed. "Honey, that kitty is gone. If the workers on the first shift didn't chase it away, the tourists did. Don't worry, Ruby is gone."

Later that night when he was making his rounds, Zira heard a trilling noise and felt something rubbing against his leg. It was the kitten!

"So — you did come back!" Zira tried to hide his pleasure. "I thought I told you to get lost."

"Meow! Meow!"

"Are you telling me you're hungry? Well, come on. I'll give you something." Ruby was in the office and on the desk as soon as Zira opened the door. She meowed loudly as she watched him pour a little milk into the thermos cup. Half of it was gone before she spied his chicken. Zira found himself feeding the kitten his supper again. Once it was gone, Ruby washed her face and curled into a ball to take a nap.

The kitten returned the next night and the next. On the fourth evening, Zira found Ruby waiting for him when he drove into the parking lot. He had a hard time trying to walk once he stepped from his car. She twisted herself around his legs and rolled on the ground in front of him until he picked her up and petted her.

Friday and Saturday were Zira's days off. He worried about the cat and hoped it would find something to eat. When he returned on Sunday, Ruby was not waiting in her usual spot. Zira

Zira heard a trilling noise at his feet. It was the kitten!

walked across the garden calling her and clapping his hands. Ruby usually came when he clapped for her, but not tonight.

Zira had an empty feeling in the pit of his stomach he could not explain. The nights were long and boring when he was alone. Did the time really go faster when Ruby was around, or did he just imagine it did? The thought of something happening to Ruby bothered him. Flashlight in hand, he decided to look for her.

He was near the east wall when he heard a muffled noise from overhead. Zira beamed the light upward. Perched on top of the high stone wall, Ruby was staring down at him.

"How did you get up there? That wall is over eight feet tall!" Ruby swished her tail back and forth, looking off into the distance. "Well, if you are going to be independent, I'll leave you there." Zira walked on down the path. To his surprise, Ruby kept pace with him up on the wall. She stopped when he stopped. He smiled at the idea of the cat walking the rounds with him like a guard dog, but she was! "Ruby, you are something else," he mumbled softly.

When they came to the end of the wall near the office, the kitten meowed loudly. "What is the matter? Can't you get down?" Before Zira could move, Ruby had leaped to a branch on the huge live oak tree and was on the ground heading for the door. She wanted her supper.

And so Ruby became a regular uninvited visitor. Each morning when Zira got off duty, the cat vanished to reappear when he returned at midnight. He wondered where Ruby spent her days. Zira told several of the Rangers on the second shift that he had a kitty, but no one believed him. He assumed Ruby left the grounds when he went home.

One evening Zira arrived for work a few minutes early. José, the security guard he was replacing, spoke of a strange squirrel that had been seen in the trees.

8

"What kind of squirrel?" Zira asked.

"It is not a regular one. It sort of flies from tree to tree," José explained. "You know most squirrels hunt for food in the daytime, but this one comes to life in the evening. No one sees it until after the gates are locked and the tourists are gone."

Later that night, when Zira started his rounds, he watched Ruby leap from a tree branch to the top of the wall. She almost seemed to be flying. Could Ruby be the "strange squirrel"?

The next morning, after Zira punched the time clock to get off duty, he walked to the Daughters of the Republic of Texas Research Library. All of the librarians were his friends, but today he wanted to talk to Margaret and Kathy. They knew a great deal about animals. Maybe they would have some suggestions on what he should do about Ruby.

After a brief exchange of greetings, Zira cleared his throat. His face was serious. "I have a problem. Will you help me?"

"We can try," Kathy replied.

Zira looked from one to the other as he said, "How can I get rid of a cat?"

Margaret smiled at the question. "Just shoo it away, I guess."

"And if it doesn't go?"

"You keep it! Why?" Kathy asked. "Do you have a cat you don't want?"

"Well," Zira stammered slowly. "It is just a little kitten. I can't seem to get rid of it. You see, I can't take it home and it doesn't want to leave."

Margaret tried to hide her smile. "What color is it?"

"Calico."

"Calico? Say, are you talking about Kensey's kitten? Does it have big green eyes?" Margaret asked.

Zira nodded his head slowly. "Yes, but I didn't know anyone else had seen it. I haven't talked to Kensey, but I have told some of the other guards that I have a kitty. They didn't believe me."

Zira watched Ruby leap to a tree branch. The cat seemed to fly through the air. Zira wondered if the Rangers could have mistaken her for the "strange squirrel."

"You should talk to Kensey. Last week the Daughters of the Republic gave him permission to keep that kitten on the grounds. Isn't that nice? There's only one thing — that cat must have shots or it won't be allowed to stay."

"Margaret is right. It must be taken to a veterinarian to be inoculated against feline enteritis," Kathy declared.

"Fe-line en-te-ri-tis?" Zira repeated slowly. "What is that?"

"That is a deadly contagious disease that kills cats. One sick animal can infect others. I don't know how we will capture the kitten to get it to the vet, though. It is scared of all of us. Kensey can get near it, but he's the only one. I have seen it in the trees, but the poor thing won't let me touch it — not yet anyway."

"Well, I'll be!" Zira muttered sheepishly. "And here I've been worrying about that kitten for nothing. It's all right for Ruby to stay."

"Ruby?" Kathy asked.

"That's what I call it. Say — why can't I take the kitty to the vet?"

Margaret's eyes shone brightly. "Could you? I will bring a case for you to carry it in. Most cats don't like to ride in a car. By the way, I'm lending Kensey a book about cats. Maybe you would like to read it when he finishes. Since this is his day off, you can talk to Kensey tomorrow."

"Thanks, I will." Zira drove home feeling a weight had been lifted from his shoulders. Now it was all right for Ruby to live in the garden and be the Alamo cat.

2

A New Home

Zira talked to Kensey before the week was over. They had a good laugh over "their" kitten and agreed Ruby was pretty special. After reading Margaret's book about cats, they understood why it was important to take the kitten to the veterinarian as soon as possible.

Ruby looked healthy. Her eyes were clear and bright, her coat was soft and silky, her nose cool and moist. But yearly vaccinations would keep Ruby from having diseases such as rabies and distemper. The day Margaret brought the carrying case, Zira made arrangements to get Ruby to a doctor.

Dr. Jones's first question was, "What is the cat's name?"

"It may be Rubin," Zira stammered, "but I call it Ruby."

The veterinarian smiled. "A calico cat is usually female — a male calico is very rare. In fact, I don't recall ever seeing a male calico." He examined the kitten while he talked. "You can go on calling her Ruby. She's a female."

"Say, I had better warn you that she bites and scratches. You should be careful, doctor. Whatever you do, don't pick her up and walk with her. She hates it. She only lets Kensey or me carry her."

The veterinarian nodded. "I always say you don't own a cat, it owns you. Cats are very independent."

Ruby scarcely blinked her eyes while the doctor checked her teeth, flashed his light down her throat, and punched her stomach. But when he reached for the needle, she moved back. "Maybe you had better hold her with both hands. This will hurt."

Zira felt the kitten flinch when the needle went into her hip, but she made no sound. The doctor lifted her into the carrying case and washed his hands.

"That is not just any old alley kitten you have there," Dr. Jones said. "She will probably always be small for her age. She could have been the runt of her litter. Ruby will make you a good pet. If you don't want her to have kittens, bring her back in four or five months. She is too young to spay now. Remember, she should have her shots once a year."

"Don't worry, doctor. We'll be back. The DRT ladies were nice enough to let Ruby stay at the Alamo, but they insisted she be vaccinated regularly."

Zira paid the doctor and carried Ruby to the car. She was going to his apartment to spend the day. They had gone a few blocks when Zira realized Ruby was deadly quiet.

"You all right, kitty?" he said, peering into the cage. The kitten was cowered in one corner with a woebegone look on her face. When they stopped for the next red light, Zira unlatched the cage and took her out. "Now you stay here on the seat by me and behave yourself. You hear?" Ruby snuggled against his leg, ignoring the traffic noises around them.

Zira's wife was waiting at the door when they drove up. Katee had heard so much about the kitten, she was eager to see Ruby for herself.

13

"Remember she scratches, honey, be careful," Zira said as he took the cat out of the cage. "She is kind of nervous, so don't try to pick her up." Zira need not have worried. After a brief examination of the apartment, Ruby seemed at home.

"She will be all right, honey. You go on to bed now and get some sleep. You look tired." Once Zira was gone, Ruby sat by the kitchen door, watching Katee wash the breakfast dishes. When she finished, Ruby followed her to the living room. Zira awoke that afternoon to find the kitten in his favorite chair. She crawled up in Katee's lap before the evening was over. "You were right, Zira. Ruby is a special kitty. I wish we could keep her."

"So do I, honey, but I'm not sure Ruby would make a good house cat. She likes to climb trees and be outdoors. Besides, I don't think Kensey would be very happy if we kept her. I know he would like to take her home, but he lives in an apartment too. This way Ruby belongs to everyone — she's the Alamo cat."

Shortly after her trip to the veterinarian, Ruby made friends with the squirrels. It was difficult to tell them apart as they sailed from limb to limb. They chased each other up one tree and down another during the cool of the mornings. The squirrels sometimes chattered so loudly the tourists stopped and watched them.

Ruby looked for a cool place to rest during the hot afternoons. She could usually be found in the flower beds or on a branch of the oak tree. Many visitors came and went never knowing Ruby was watching them from her hiding place high above the ground. She was difficult to see. Her white, black, and reddish-orange coloring blended with the leaves and bark on the limbs. Occasionally, an observant person caught sight of Ruby's legs dangling in the air as she stretched out on her stomach across a bough.

As the days went by, Ruby grew more daring. She no longer

When she was in a playful mood, Ruby chased the butterflies.

ran from the workers who walked across the Alamo grounds on their way to the various buildings. She let them pet her, but they learned not to pick her up. The ones who tried dropped her in a hurry. Her teeth were sharp!

When she was in a playful mood, Ruby sometimes entertained the tourists by chasing the butterflies across the flower beds. The gardeners complained she was ruining their petunias, but they were teasing. The petunias, like the irises, roses, and bluebonnets, were only flowers. But Ruby was the mascot of the Alamo.

The Rangers patrolled the gardens inside the gates as well as the grounds in front of the Alamo wall. Like policemen patrolling their beats, they walked their rounds. One evening as Zira unlocked the outside gate, the kitten was at his heels. "No, Ruby, you stay here. You must not follow me. It is time you learned to obey commands — if a dog can learn, so can you. Now, sit!" He pushed her bottom to the ground. "Now you sit right there by the gate. I'll be back in a minute."

Ruby cocked her head to one side and watched him walk away. When he reached the edge of the wall, Zira looked back. Ruby was peeking at him around the gate, but she had not moved.

Zira was surprised at how quickly Ruby learned. When they came to the outer gate he always shook his finger at her. "Sit right there, kitty." Although she peered at him around the corner of the wall, Ruby did not try to follow him again.

The Rangers kept an eye on Ruby during the day as they patrolled the grounds and answered the visitors' questions. One of Ruby's favorite tricks was hiding behind a bush until someone walked by. Then — without warning — she grabbed the unsuspecting person's ankle and would be gone before they could catch her.

16

Ruby particularly delighted in surprising the librarians when they walked through the garden on their way to work. Margaret and Kathy learned to watch for her as they neared a certain bush beside the water ditch. They knew Ruby would be waiting to surprise them as they passed by. But they did not mind her tricks — Ruby was just a frisky, playful kitten.

3

Ruby's Big Surprise

As the weeks flew by, fall gave way to the chill of winter. One cold December evening, Zira and Ruby were making their regular rounds. As they neared the museum, Ruby stopped and hunched her back the way she did when there was danger.

"What do you see, kitty?" Zira whispered softly. He shined his flashlight slowly over the bushes in front of them. "What is —"

Before Zira could finish, a deep snarling sound came from Ruby's throat. With a wild look in her eyes, she sprang forward. The silence was suddenly broken by the savage noise of battle. Ruby was fighting tooth and claw with some animal.

As Zira raced to her rescue, a scrawny yellow cat streaked across his path. Ruby was in hot pursuit. Zira took off after Ruby. They chased the yellow cat until it vanished into the shadows outside the grounds. Finally satisfied the creature was gone, Ruby turned back.

"Meow!" she cried proudly, twisting herself around Zira's legs. She would not stop until he picked her up.

"You think you're pretty smart, don't you?" Ruby rubbed her head against Zira's chin as he carried her across the courtyard to the office. Once they were inside, Zira made sure the kitten was all right. He shook his head. "You were lucky you were not hurt this time, but don't you do that again. You hear?"

With a smug look on her face, Ruby stretched across the desk and closed her eyes. Zira stroked her absent-mindedly. Suddenly, he looked at her more closely.

"Ruby, are you getting fat?" He realized she was no longer a tiny ball of fluff. She had grown sleek and plump. Zira chuckled softly as he playfully swished her tail from side to side. "I'd say you are too big to be a kitten anymore, but you're too small to be a cat."

A few days later, Kensey met Zira as he was leaving. "I hoped I could catch you before you went home. I have some news for you. You know our kitty only lets us pick her up?"

"That's the truth!"

"Well, yesterday Ruby was sleeping near the path in the garden. I guess she didn't see the lady until it was too late. The first thing I knew the woman had Ruby in her arms. I could not stop her. But, for once, Ruby did not bite. You know what that woman said?"

Zira shook his head.

"Ruby is going to have kittens!"

"Why, she can't do that!" Zira declared with a shocked look on his face. "She's just a baby herself! Besides, how would that woman know?"

Kensey laughed. "Funny, that is exactly what I said!"

"And it's a fact!"

"I told the woman Ruby was too young to have kittens — she's less than six months old! But when I learned she was a vet-

With a smug look on her face, Ruby stretched across the desk and closed her eyes.

erinarian, I figured the woman knew what she was talking about!"

"A veterinarian?"

"Yes, and she said we could expect Ruby to have a family in a couple of weeks — that would be around the first of February. And that's not all."

"Oh?"

"The librarians have done some research. It seems when Ruby's kittens are born they will be the first babies ever recorded at the Alamo!"

"Well, I'll be!" Zira walked off mumbling to himself.

The news of Ruby's babies spread quickly to workers in the museum and the curator's office. Once they heard, everyone brought food to the mother-to-be. Ruby welcomed their treats at first. But, with so much to eat, she soon became finicky. She turned up her nose at milk and walked away from fish in disgust. Ruby let them know she was a particular cat. She ate only what she liked. But by midnight, when Zira came to work, Ruby was ready to share his snack.

Each evening when the sun went down and the second shift of Rangers toured the grounds, Ruby waited by the back gate for Zira. He, in turn, looked for her when he drove into the parking lot. Ruby had become an important part of his life.

When Katee learned Ruby was expecting kittens, she said, "You must make her a bed. Ruby needs to have a warm one in a place where there are no drafts. If they are due in February we could still have cold weather. We don't want them to get sick, do we?"

"No . . ."

"And once you get the bed made, we'll line it with newspapers. I'll get Ruby a blanket. Most animals like a clean, quiet place to have their babies. After they are born, you must change the papers to keep the bed nice and fresh."

Zira bought the things he needed to make Ruby's bed. When it was finished, he carried it to the Long Barracks and placed it in a dark, warm corner. Ruby investigated the boxlike bed carefully, but she refused to stay in it. Zira carried her back to the corner several times, but she would not stay.

"Ruby, I went to a lot of trouble making that for you. Don't you like it?" Waving her tail back and forth, Ruby arched her back and rubbed against his legs. "I guess Katee was right. She said you might not pay attention to it until it was time for you to have your babies." Ruby purred loudly as he scratched her back.

During the winter nights that followed, Ruby continued making the rounds with Zira. No amount of scolding made her change her mind about climbing the trees. Zira constantly shook his finger at her. "Ruby, you are getting too fat. You must be careful!"

The kitten did not understand what was happening to her. One night she started through the metal gate ahead of Zira the way she always did. Without warning, she found herself wedged between the bars. She discovered she could not move forward or backward. She was stuck! Ruby meowed loudly until Zira came to get her loose. After that, Ruby let him unlatch the gate. Once it was open, she sat near the wall of the Alamo and waited for Zira to return.

As the time grew closer for Ruby to have her babies, she catnapped more and more. At night Zira watched her closely. Kensey kept an eye on Ruby during the daytime when he was on duty. He promised Zira he would call if Ruby's kittens were born during his shift.

One morning Zira said, "Better watch Ruby today, Kensey.

She acted kind of strange last night. She seemed restless and nervous."

Zira worried about Ruby all the way home. The minute he walked into his apartment the telephone started ringing.

"Hello," he said.

"This is Kensey. I just called to tell you that Ruby had a kitten. It is black but it only has a stump of a tail! I'll call you if she has another one."

Zira got little sleep after that. The telephone kept ringing. Before the day was over, Ruby had six kittens — and half of them had no tails! When Zira heard that, he forgot about sleep. He and Katee wanted to see the kittens.

When they reached the Alamo, everyone was in a dither. In the excitement someone had called the local newspaper office. A photographer was there snapping pictures of Ruby and her kittens for the morning paper. The reporter said he was an authority on cats. Zira wondered if he was right when he said Ruby had four males and two females. Ruby was not happy when the reporter picked up her kittens to examine them.

Once the television station heard the news, a camera crew rushed to the Alamo to get a report for the evening news. The crew had to bring in special lighting to take pictures of Ruby and her kittens in the dark corner of the Long Barracks.

Ruby was totally unconcerned about all the activity around her. She went about the business of grooming and caring for her new family. The mother cat curled around the kittens to keep them warm and to let them nurse. Ruby did not seem to realize — or care — that she was getting so much publicity.

The next day someone suggested birth announcements be sent to the DRT ladies. "That's a wonderful idea!" Kensey said. "After all, they were kind enough to let us keep Ruby. I am sure they would like to know about the first babies ever born inside the Alamo grounds. Ruby is history in the making."

The Rangers in the office agreed it would be nice to send out announcements. "But shouldn't the kittens have names?" someone asked.

Kensey grinned at the thought. "Say, that's a good idea too. I will talk to Zira about naming them for the heroes of the Alamo."

"We could call them Bonham or Bowie or Crockett," one of the men said.

Another Ranger spoke up, "I think it would be good to name one of them after John McGregor, the Scotchman."

"Why couldn't they have double names like Bowie Bonham?"

Kensey nodded. "All of those are fine suggestions."

"But what about the two females?" one of the guards asked. "What will they be named?"

"I had forgotten about them," Kensey said slowly. "I guess I had better talk to the librarians."

Margaret thought of a perfect solution. "One kitten could be named Susanna Angelina after Mrs. Dickinson and her baby daughter. The other could be Gertrudes Juanita or *Señora* Esparza. I like the first one best."

"I think you have the answer, Margaret. I will call Zira while I'm on my coffee break and see what he thinks." Zira liked the names too.

Later, Kensey learned that Kathy spent her lunch hour trying to design a card. He hurried to the drug store across the street to buy a baby announcement to use as a guide. With that as a model, Kathy typed a similar card for Ruby's family. She insisted the kittens names should not be typed but written by hand.

Someone said Ruby needed a last name. Everyone agreed Le Gato was perfect. *"Gato"* is the Spanish word for cat. The librarians decided the names of the two godfathers — Zira and Kensey — should also be included on the announcements.

"How are we going to know how much they weigh?" Margaret asked. "We can't leave that space on the card blank, can we?"

"I've been worrying about addressing and writing in all those names," Kathy said. "We would never get them finished on our lunch hour."

"Why don't we divide them up so we can work on them at home tonight? That way we could have them ready to mail tomorrow."

"That's a good suggestion, Margaret. Do you think Kensey could weigh one of the kittens on our postage scales before we leave?" Kathy asked.

Kensey laughed at the idea. "I can try. I just hope the new mother doesn't mind us handling her babies." Ruby had a nervous gleam in her eyes as she watched him balance one of her kittens on the scales. "It weighs six ounces," Kensey said as he put the baby back. "Don't worry, Ruby, I won't weigh all six of them. We will say they all weigh about six ounces."

The librarians spent the evening working on the cards. After the announcements were mailed the next day, the kittens started receiving guests. Among the first was Carol, one of the newer librarians. She presented Ruby with a guest book to keep a record of the visitors. "After all," Carol declared, "that information might someday be written in a book."

With all the excitement, Zira worried that someone might step on one of the tiny kittens. He put a cardboard fence around Ruby's bed to protect them. Everyone called that corner the nursery.

The visitors asked all sorts of questions. Kensey reread Margaret's book about cats so he could answer them. Everyone kept asking, "When will they open their eyes?"

Announcing the Arrival

Susanna Angelina, Barret Butler,
Gertrudes Juanita, Zanco McGregor,
OF Bowie Crockett, Micajah Galba

BORN ON 2 February 1982

WEIGHT 6 oz. each (approx.)

PARENTS Ruby LeGato — Mother

Rue "Pepe" LeGato — Father

Godfathers - Zira
Kensey

Birth announcements were sent to the Daughters of the Republic of Texas.

"Well," Kensey replied, "the book says they will be opened by the ninth day. Did you know they can't smell or taste or hear until they are about three days old?"

The first visitors went away shaking their heads. It was strange to see Ruby, who was just a kitten herself, with six little babies.

4

Ruby's Kittens

The excitement over Ruby's kittens gradually settled down. Things at the Alamo returned to normal for everyone but Zira. He missed having Ruby walk guard with him. Each morning after he cleaned her bed, he lingered around long enough to swap stories with some of the other Rangers. Ruby had surprised them all by the way she assumed the role of motherhood at her young age.

Zira's wife was full of questions when he finally got home. "How's Ruby? Are the kittens getting plenty to eat?"

"You should see them, honey. They are getting fat!"

"Are you sure Ruby has fresh water every day? Nursing so many kittens she needs it. Are you sure they are warm enough?"

"You don't have to worry, honey," Zira laughed. "Everyone is keeping an eye on those kittens."

Ruby was too busy to notice anything. She washed each baby a dozen times a day to be sure it was clean. If one rolled away from the others, Ruby moved it back with her paw. She cuddled them together against her body to keep them warm. Like most animal mothers, Ruby instinctively knew how to protect and care for her little ones.

Zira worried that Ruby might try to follow him out the door as he went to make his nightly rounds. Little did he know Ruby had no thought of leaving her family — not even to walk guard with him.

The Long Barracks office was a popular place for the Rangers during their lunch hours and coffee breaks. At those times other employees also dropped by to chat and to see Ruby. Kensey always called their attention to the way the kittens were growing.

"See how they are changing? Most of them have their eyes opened now."

"Yes, and they are crawling about and tumbling over each other," someone said. "But look at that little fellow — the one with four white socks. He's much smaller than the others."

"Yes," Kensey said, "And they bully him around too. The librarians call him Barret Butler Baby."

"Poor thing, he seems to always be at the bottom of the pile."

"Don't worry," Kensey replied. "Ruby makes sure he is not mistreated. She is a good mother."

"How can you tell them apart?" one of the men asked.

"Sometimes I can't. The two females are calico-colored like Ruby. Bowie Crockett is that biggest one. He is coal black with a stubby tail."

"And the little one is Barret Butler?"

Kensey nodded his head. "That's right. Those two black-and-white ones are exactly alike except one has a tail and the other doesn't. They are Zanco McGregor and Micajah Galba."

29

Ruby and her six babies had many visitors.

"Their names are bigger than they are," one of the men chuckled.

It was surprising how the kittens changed daily. Bowie Crockett was the first to open his eyes. The others opened theirs a short time later. Bowie Crockett was also the first to stagger on his wobbly legs to the far corner of the box. When he could not find his way back to his mother, he began to yell. He woke up the others with his racket and made them cry. Ruby had a time getting all six of them quietened down again.

Kathy and Margaret were regular visitors during the lunch hour. "The afternoon seems to go faster after we've been to see Ruby," Kathy said one day. "Watching those kittens is like watching a three-ring circus. Something is happening in every corner."

"You're right," Margaret said. "Look at Bowie Crockett. One minute he's crawling on Ruby's head and the next he's chasing her tail."

"Just look at Susanna Angelina. She is sitting on her sister!" Kathy laughed.

The Rangers crowded around to watch. "Poor Ruby needs six pairs of eyes to keep up with them. Barret Butler Baby is the only one not causing trouble. He's asleep," Margaret said. The smallest kitten was sprawled out on his back with his little legs straight up in the air.

Kensey shook his head. "They won't let him sleep for long." As he talked, the two black-and-white kittens were crawling around over Ruby's back, chasing each other. Suddenly, one lost his footing and rolled down his mother's stomach. He landed in the middle of little Barret Butler, who woke up squalling. Everyone laughed — but Ruby did not find it funny.

The days passed quickly. By the time the kittens were four weeks old, Bowie Crockett was the strongest. He spent his waking moments pushing and shoving the others around. One eve-

31

ning Zira heard an awful racket coming from the box. It did not take him long to find the cause. The five smaller kittens were crying because Bowie Crockett had shoved them away so they could not nurse.

"Shame on you, Bowie. You're just a bully," Zira scolded. "Little mother, you ought to teach that fellow some manners." Poor Ruby was too tired to care. Keeping up with six hungry babies day and night was no easy task.

One evening Zira opened the office door and stumbled over Bowie Crockett.

"Say, how did you get out?" Zira put the kitten back with Ruby and sat down at his desk to make his report. When Zira looked up a few minutes later, he was surprised to see Bowie Crockett in the middle of the floor again.

"What is this?" he muttered, carrying the kitten back once more. Bowie Crockett crawled over the fence before Zira could sit down. "Well, if you won't stay in your bed we are going to have trouble. It won't be long before all of those kittens will be out too." Zira shook his head.

A few days later, Kensey met the librarians on their way to work. After the three of them discussed the weather, Kathy's face grew serious. "We have been talking about Ruby and the kittens. Have you and Zira decided what to do with them?"

Kensey shook his head slowly.

"Well, since neither you nor Zira can take them home, it is something you must face. Just look how they have grown in six weeks."

"That's a fact! They are everywhere. Margaret, did you say you would take a kitten?"

She nodded. "My husband agreed I could have not one but two! They will keep each other company. I would like to have Barret Butler — the little one — and maybe Bowie Crockett."

"One of the DRT ladies said she would like two of them. That leaves only two that need homes," Kathy said.

Kensey sighed deeply. "When will they be old enough to leave Ruby?"

"They all probably have their baby teeth by now since they are nibbling at solid food. Don't worry — Ruby will let you know when it is time to give them away. She will start weaning them." With a half smile Margaret added, "Nature has a wonderful way of taking care of those things. I would say you can plan on giving them away in a week or so. They will be almost two months old by then."

"Ruby wasn't that old when she came, was she?"

"But remember, Kensey, Ruby was probably dumped. That is a cruel way to get rid of unwanted animals." Margaret shook her head at the thought. "Oh, that brings us to something else. It is time to make arrangements to spay Ruby so she won't have more babies."

"Why, she couldn't have another family — not this soon." Kensey was startled at the idea.

"Yes, she could," Margaret's face was solemn.

Kathy nodded. "And she just might if you don't get her to the veterinarian soon."

Kensey immediately called Zira. They agreed it would be disastrous for Ruby to have another family. The office was already full of wiggly, squirmy, playful kittens. They certainly did not need another litter — not now. After talking to Kensey, Zira called the veterinarian.

"You can bring her in tomorrow."

"Are you sure she will be all right? She has kittens, you know," Zira said.

"Don't worry. It is a simple procedure. She won't feel a thing."

"Are you sure?"

The doctor laughed into the telephone. "We will put her to sleep and make a small incision on her abdomen. That's all. She will be fine."

After the operation, Ruby continued to bathe and care for her kittens while she weaned them. Once they were eating regular food, it was amazing how quickly things changed in the Long Barracks. Margaret put Barret Bonham and Bowie Crockett into her carrying case and took them home. Two other kittens went home with the DRT lady. Zira gave one to Ranger José for his little girl. A friend of Kensey's asked for the other female. After the kittens were gone, the office seemed strangely silent.

Zira worried that Ruby might grieve. With an uninterested look in her eyes, she watched him remove the cardboard fence. Soon all traces of the kittens and the nursery were gone. If Ruby missed them, she gave no sign. It was as if the experience had never happened as she walked the rounds with Zira. He was happy to have Ruby once more serve as guard cat of the Alamo.

5

Danger!

The warm days of spring gave way to the heat of summer. Without the burdens of motherhood, Ruby returned to her old tricks.

She darted in and out among the branches and played with the squirrels. She hid behind the bushes to surprise some unsuspecting person who chanced along. Margaret and Kathy expected Ruby to be waiting to grab their ankles when they neared the bush by the water ditch. The Rangers could usually find her napping in a shady corner of the flower bed during the hot afternoons.

Everyone agreed it was good having Ruby back to normal. They had missed her.

Many different kinds of birds made their nests in the trees of the Alamo garden. Ruby watched them with interest. One day she surprised Kensey by laying a dead bird at his feet.

"Ruby! Did you kill that baby bird?" Kensey scolded. "Shame on you! You leave them alone, you hear?"

Ruby cocked her head to one side and stared at him. He had never talked to her like that. She did not like it. Kensey could not keep from laughing. "Ruby, you can almost talk!"

Ruby knew he was laughing at her. She did not think it was funny. With her nose high in the air, Ruby raised her tail upright and stalked away. She was near the bridge over the *acequia* when two mockingbirds suddenly appeared from a nearby tree. They dived straight at Ruby's head. Caught completely by surprise, the cat lost her footing and fell backward into the water ditch. Kensey saw her falling and rushed to the edge of the ditch. He grabbed her by the neck and pulled her out.

"See? You killed a bird and now the mockingbirds are after you. You had better stay away from their nests. You hear?"

Ruby shivered with fear as he dried her off. Once Kensey put her down, she was gone. No one saw her again that day. She was hiding. Ruby avoided that spot by the *acequia* for days.

During the summer months, thousands of tourists visited the Alamo grounds. The Rangers gave them directions and answered all sorts of questions. In addition to those duties, Kensey and the other Rangers made certain no one walked on the grass or picked the flowers. But, in spite of the regulations, the visitors looked for souvenirs to take home — a rock or leaf or stick.

One afternoon Kensey happened around the corner of the library in time to stop a woman from taking Ruby! "Lady," he declared angrily as he took Ruby from her arms. "This is our cat!"

"It is?"

"It most certainly is!"

The woman replied shamefacedly, "It doesn't have a collar. I thought it was a stray."

"Well, she's not," Kensey said, lifting Ruby up to a low branch of a nearby tree. He watched until she disappeared

Ruby fell into the water ditch when the mockingbird dived at her.

Ruby was dripping wet when Kensey pulled her from the water.

among the leaves on an upper limb, then he gave the woman a cold stare. "Did you know there are laws about defacing or harming the state's property?"

"Well . . ."

"And that includes the birds and squirrels and our cat!"

The woman apologized half-heartedly and hurried away.

When Zira heard what had happened and that they had almost lost Ruby, he was furious. "Maybe we had better put a name tag on her."

"Good idea," Kensey agreed. "But with her climbing trees the way she does, isn't there a danger of her getting caught on one of the branches? If she did she could get choked."

"I hadn't thought of that," Zira said thoughtfully. "Maybe I had better call the doctor and see what he says."

The veterinarian recommended one of the newer expansion collars. Ruby was not overjoyed with the idea of a necklace, but she got used to wearing it.

6

Ruby Defends the Alamo

The year of 1986 started with a bang! Skies over the Alamo blazed with a fireworks display that marked the beginning of the year-long celebration of Texas's sesquicentennial. At the stroke of midnight a thunderous roar went up from the huge throng of people assembled in Alamo Plaza.

From her hiding place in the old oak tree, Ruby stared down at the crowd. She did not understand the New Year's party was to celebrate the state's 150 years of independence from Mexico. Ruby only knew Zira was too busy that night to pay attention to her.

In the days and weeks that followed, many people visited the Alamo. Some were dressed in unusual costumes. They wore pioneer clothing or western garb or brightly colored *serapes* like the people of bygone days wore. Perched on her branch in the oak tree, Ruby had a panoramic view of the ceremonies during Texas's Independence Week, which started the first of March. She

The branch on the oak tree was Ruby's favorite resting place.

did not want to be part of the crowd of tourists milling around the grounds. But when the Rangers took their coffee breaks, she joined them in the Long Barracks office. That was her time to beg for food.

One afternoon she rubbed against Kensey's leg, begging him to pick her up. "I know your tricks, kitty. You only come to me when you are hungry. Everybody knows you walk guard with Zira when he's on duty. You are just a one-man cat."

"What do you mean by that?" one of the newer Rangers asked.

Kensey chuckled softly. "I can see you don't know Ruby."

"What's wrong with her?"

"Nothing. It is just that she tolerates the rest of us but she loves Zira. Why, I think this cat would risk her life for Zira if she had to."

Everyone laughed. They had no way of knowing that Ruby would prove the truth of Kensey's words.

In the wee hours of the morning, a few weeks later, Zira walked out of the library after checking the windows. A sharp wind caused him to turn up the collar of his jacket. He locked the door and turned around to look for Ruby. She was not allowed inside the library, but she usually waited for him near the fountain. She was not there.

"Ruby? Where are you?" Zira flashed his light along the sidewalk. There was no sign of her. When he clapped his hands, Ruby usually came on the run — but not tonight.

Sensing an unseen danger, Zira felt a cold chill run up his spine. He zigzagged the light slowly across the flower beds to his right. There was still no sign of Ruby. He moved the beam slowly along the path to the bushes near the water ditch. Then he saw her. She was poised for attack.

At that moment Zira saw something that made his blood run

Ruby was ready to attack the raccoon, which was twice her size.

cold. A huge raccoon twice Ruby's size was waiting for her. Zira realized Ruby's small claws and teeth would be no defense against the more powerful animal. Raccoons are famous for luring other animals into a fight near water. By skillful maneuvering, they could make their opponent stumble backward into a ditch. In a flash, the raccoon would be into the water. It would hold the other animal's head under water as it struggled and finally drowned.

Zira knew he had to act quickly to stop Ruby before it was too late. He took a deep breath and, with a mighty lunge, wrapped his arms around the cat before she could move. Ruby hissed and spit in protest, but Zira held on.

"Now, settle down, Ruby," he whispered softly. "That animal could kill you! Just look at him — he looks mean enough to try to attack me! Now, simmer down while I think of a way to get that critter out of here."

Zira rubbed Ruby's chin to calm her as he thought of some way to catch the raccoon by surprise. There was only one thing to do — run straight toward the animal! Zira shifted the cat to his other arm as he reached for his flashlight, which had fallen to the ground. "Kitty, let's see if we can scare him out. Here we go!"

Zira gave a wild yell and leaped straight at the raccoon. The animal was caught completely off guard. It crept backward a few steps, then suddenly turned to flee toward the back entrance. Zira was right behind. The animal disappeared into the darkness as it reached the rear gate. Zira flashed the light up and down the empty, silent street. The raccoon was nowhere in sight.

With a sigh of relief, Zira turned toward the Long Barracks. He dared not let Ruby down. She might dash off looking for the creature.

"We'll get something to eat, kitty. Then I'll leave you inside for a while." Once they were in the office, Zira put Ruby on the desk and slipped off his jacket. Ruby's sharp claws had ripped his coat, but Zira did not care. Ruby had risked her life to defend the Alamo, but now she was safe.

The next morning the Rangers gathered around to hear Zira's story. He was holding Ruby, and she rubbed her head against Zira's chin as he talked. "You fellows should have been here last night. We had an intruder!"

"What kind?" someone asked.

"A fierce-looking raccoon about twice Ruby's size!"

Kensey's eyes were round in wonder. "Those creatures can be dangerous."

"Yes, and you should have seen Ruby — she was ready to fight that critter to defend the Alamo! I tell you she is a real guard cat."

Kensey chuckled softly as he patted Ruby's head. "But the question is — was Ruby defending the Alamo, or was she defending you, Zira?"

Everyone smiled.

"Fellows, it might be a good idea to keep an eye on Ruby in case that raccoon comes back."

"Do you think it might?" Kensey asked seriously.

"There is no way of knowing where it came from. It could be holed up on those streets back behind the Alamo where they are tearing out those old buildings," Zira declared.

"You could be right."

"Anyway, I'm going to be gone for a few days. I won't be back until Sunday night. How about passing the word along to the other shift and to the fellow who will take my place? Tell them to keep an eye on Ruby for me." Zira glanced at the clock and headed for the door. "I guess I had better get home or my wife will be worrying about me." With a wave of his hand, Zira walked out of the office and headed for the parking lot.

When he returned to work Sunday, Zira knew something was wrong. Kensey was waiting for him by the gate.

"What is it? Why are you here at this hour of the night?"

"Well," Kensey sounded hoarse. He found it difficult to talk for the lump in his throat. "I wanted to be the one to tell you. Ruby is gone."

"Gone?"

"The boys found her in the water ditch. She drowned!"

"Drowned? How? She had fallen into the *acequia* before, but she always got out."

Kensey shook his head slowly. "No one knows how it happened. Some think the mockingbirds were after her again and that they frightened her to the deepest spot by the north wall. That's where they found her body. Others say that raccoon came back and that it somehow pulled her into the water. They think the raccoon drowned her. But I guess we will never know for sure. The DRT ladies gave us permission to bury Ruby here by the north corner of the wall."

Zira stared down at the small grave in silence. Someone had made a wooden marker and written the words

RUBY, The Alamo Cat
1981–1986

Kensey sighed deeply as he said, "Perhaps we can get another cat."

Zira shook his head. "There will never be another Ruby." His shoulders slumped. He walked away slowly.

As if awakening from a dream, Zira returned to the present. Bright patches of moonlight dotted the ground where the light filtered through the leaves. Still staring down into the murky waters, Zira sighed and straightened his shoulders.

Although Zira has accepted the fact that Ruby is gone, he knows her spirit lives on in the hearts of those who loved her. Love never dies — it has no ending. Ruby was — and will always be — the Alamo cat.

Today Ruby's grave has a concrete slab and a marble marker with a Texas flag. She will always be the Alamo cat.

Bibliography

Adult

Gilbert, John R. *Cats, Cats, Cats, Cats.* London: Hamlyn Publishing Ltd., 1972.

James, Allen. *The Stanyan Book of Cats.* New York: Random House, 1971.

Miller, Harry. *The Common Sense Book of Kitten and Cat Care.* New York: Bantam, 1966.

Periodicals

Barneburg, Tina. "Alamo Grounds Part of Shrine." *San Antonio Express-News,* March 6, 1987.

Fehrenbach, T. R. "Alamo Remains Stirring Symbol." *San Antonio Express-News,* March 1, 1987.